This book belongs to

- -

- -

For Justin —RLO
For Pip and Lori —LB

For Tilda —David O'Connell

[Imprint]
MAKE YOUR MARK

A part of Macmillan Publishing Group, LLC
120 Broadway, New York, NY 10271

DAVE THE UNICORN: DANCE PARTY. Text copyright © 2019 by Egmont UK Ltd.
Illustrations copyright © 2019 by David O'Connell. All rights reserved. Printed in
the United States of America by LSC Communications, Harrisonburg, Virginia.

Library of Congress Control Number: 2020908606

ISBN 978-1-250-25638-6 (hardcover) / ISBN 978-1-250-25639-3 (ebook)

Our books may be purchased in bulk for promotional, educational, or
business use. Please contact your local bookseller or the Macmillan Corporate
and Premium Sales Department at (800) 221-7945 ext. 5442 or by
email at MacmillanSpecialMarkets@macmillan.com.

Book design by Lizzie Gardiner

Special thanks to Liz Bankes and Rebecca Lewis-Oakes

Imprint logo designed by Amanda Spielman

Originally published in Great Britain by Egmont UK Limited in 2019

First American edition, 2020

1 3 5 7 9 10 8 6 4 2

mackids.com

You can jump, you can jive,
But if you steal this book,
You shall not thrive!

DAVE THE UNICORN

DANCE PARTY

PIP BIRD

ILLUSTRATED BY DAVID O'CONNELL

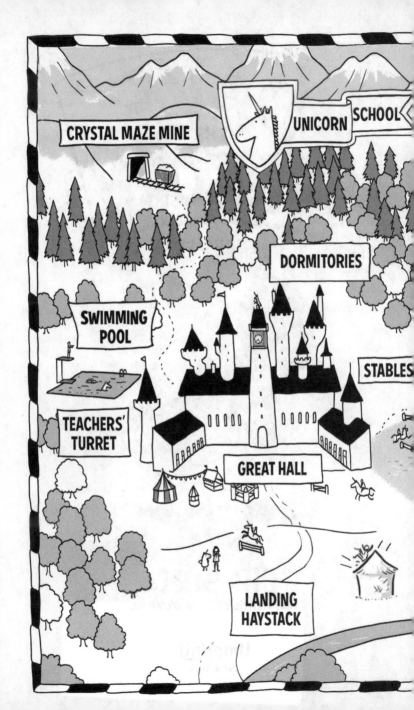

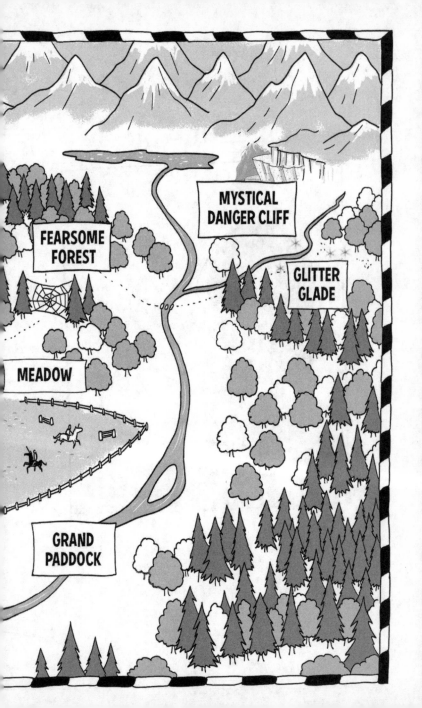

Contents

CHAPTER ONE
Back to Unicorn School!

It was a cloudy Tuesday afternoon and Mira was dancing around the kitchen with her cat, Pickles. Mira's older sister, Rani, rolled her eyes as she finished the after-dinner dishwashing (her chore for that week), and flicked water at Mira and Pickles as they twirled past the sink.

"Bleurgh!" spluttered Mira as a soap bubble landed in her mouth.

Rani dried her hands on a dish towel and snatched Pickles off Mira. "My turn! Okay,

Pickles, you can be my unicorn," she said. "I need to practice my moves for the school dance."

As Rani and Pickles swept past her, Mira had to admit that Rani was an annoyingly good dancer. Rani and her unicorn, Angelica, were annoyingly good at lots of things. The trophy shelf in their living room was full of Rani's medals and trophies from winning tons of Unicorn School quests and competitions. Mira had just two medals so far.

Mira and Rani both went to Unicorn School. It was a magical place where students were matched with their Unicorn Best Friend Forever (UBFF) and had all kinds of brilliant quests and adventures!

2

It was almost time to go back to Unicorn School, and Mira was BEYOND EXCITED to see her UBFF, Dave. He wasn't exactly how she'd imagined her perfect unicorn to be . . . He could be a little stubborn. And greedy. And he fell asleep in all their lessons. But they had so much fun together. And the school dance was going to be the most fun EVER. She couldn't imagine anything better in the entire world than spinning around the dance floor with Dave!

∪ ∪ ∪

Later that night Mira lay in bed, too excited to sleep. She took out her diary from her bedside table and started thinking about all the awesome things she was going to do with Dave. *And* with

Darcy and Raheem—her two human best friends at Unicorn School.

Going on AMAZING quests

Dance with my BFFs

Midnight feasts in the dormitory

And BEST OF ALL... DAVE, MY UBFF!!!!

Thinking about Dave made Mira smile. He always made everything super fun, often in unexpected ways. Sure, he sometimes had to be bribed with snacks to do things. And sometimes he caused a teeny, tiny bit of havoc. *And* he held the Unicorn School record for most farts in class. But he didn't *mean* to misbehave. Dave was Mira's UBFF, and she loved him.

Mira tucked her diary back in the drawer and fell asleep.

ᘮᘮᘮ

Mom usually took Mira and Rani to the Magic Portal, where they could travel to Unicorn School— but today Dad was driving them, and they had to explain *everything* to him. He even nearly forgot

to take them to the supermarket to buy treats for their unicorns! (Most unicorns liked carrots and hay, but Dave liked doughnuts best of all.)

"Stop, Dad!" yelled Mira. They were about to drive right past the Magic Portal in the rec center parking lot! Dad made an emergency stop as Mira hung out of the car, waving to her friend Raheem.

Rani refused to be seen dead (her words) with Mira at Unicorn School, so Mira had arranged to go through the portal with Raheem. He was just finishing the "Rules of Keeping Safe" song with his dad, but he did wave back.

Dad was under strict instruction to take a picture of them before they went through the  portal. Rani would only pose for a fraction of a second, but the photo of the back of her head would have to do.

"Bye, Dad!" Mira blew him a kiss through the car window and made sure she had her bag of unicorn treats. "Ready, Raheem? Why do you have your eyes closed?"

"I always feel sick going through the portal," Raheem said. "So I'm doing my calming breathing."

Mira grabbed his hand and pulled them both through the bushes. No matter how many times she went through the portal, it never stopped being absolutely, completely magical.

First, her toes started to tingle, then her legs and arms, and then rainbow light burst all around them and they were WHOOSHING through the air before landing with a soft *thump* on the Landing Haystack in the middle of the Grand Paddock at Unicorn School.

"Wow," breathed Mira as she looked around. It was autumn, and all the leaves in the Fearsome Forest were turning gorgeous shades of red and gold. Children were arriving in a steady stream on the Landing Haystack and running to find their UBFFs. The unicorns were grazing and playing in the paddocks and fields around Unicorn School.

Mira could see their breath puffing in the chilly air as she searched for Dave.

"Ta-daaaa!" a voice sang out behind them on the haystack. Their friend Darcy launched off the haystack and did a spectacular spin in her wheelchair with her arms in the air. "Did you miss me?"

Mira laughed and ran over for a hug. "Of course I missed you. That was awesome!"

Darcy flicked her fluffy blond hair back over her shoulder. "I know," she said. "I've been practicing my moves for the school dance. I started a feet-and-wheels dance troupe at my other school because I was kicked off the murderball team. They said I was too aggressive or something. Anyway, dance is WAY more my thing."

"What's murderball?" asked Raheem cautiously.

"It's like rugby but in wheelchairs. And more dangerous," Darcy replied, looking around for her unicorn, Star.

Raheem looked a little bit lost for words. "Shall we go find our unicorns?" he said.

Star and Brave were grazing in the Grand Paddock and cantered over as soon as they spotted Darcy and Raheem. Mira couldn't see Dave.

"Is that him?" asked Darcy, pointing to a giant pile of straw by the side of the fence. Some of the Unicorn School teachers were standing around it, poking something on the top of the straw pile with a stick. Mira looked closer and saw that it was a small unicorn curled up, fast asleep.

"Wake up!" yelled the PE teacher, Miss Hind.

"How is he still asleep?" muttered another teacher, shaking his head.

"He's been up there for sixteen hours!" said their class teacher, Miss Glitterhorn.

Dave farted loudly in his sleep.

Mira gave a huge smile. *There* was her UBFF. And she knew JUST how to wake him up!

Mira reached into her pocket. "Dave!" she called. "I've got a super-special treat for you!" Mira pulled out a strawberry licorice and waved it in the air.

Up on the straw pile, she was sure she could see Dave's nostrils twitching. Then he gave a loud snort and sat bolt upright. His ears pricked up, his nose twitched, and he looked down at Mira.

Dave launched himself off the top of the straw pile, bounced off Miss Hind's head, and landed in a heap just in front of Mira. Miss Hind muttered angrily to herself, but the other teachers just seemed relieved that Dave was finally awake.

Dave swallowed the strawberry licorice and

licked Mira's face. She giggled and pulled another
candy string out of her pocket.

Dave slurped up the treat, then farted happily.
Just then, the school bell rang, calling the students
and unicorns inside. It was time for Unicorn
School to begin!

CHAPTER TWO
The School Dance Committee

Madame Shetland, the Unicorn School principal, waited as everyone gathered in the hall.

"Welcome back to Unicorn School, my dear students, unicorns, and teachers," said Madame Shetland. "Today, I have two very special announcements. Firstly, this week Class Red has a very important quest. Students will be traveling to the Crystal Maze Mine to search for Warming Crystals. These crystals heat the school and keep us all warm as the weather turns colder."

Mira's classmates in Class Red started chatting excitedly. It took three teachers to shush them. Mira high-fived Darcy, who whispered loudly, "Great, but when can we talk about the dance?"

"And secondly," continued Madame Shetland, raising her voice over the noise, "as you know, we will also have a school dance. This will take place in two days' time."

Whoops and squeals of excitement echoed around the hall. Mira grinned happily. A dance AND a super important quest. Amazing!

Two loud taps came over the loudspeakers. Everyone stopped and looked around, wondering what was going on. Darcy had wheeled up to Madame Shetland's podium and taken hold of the microphone.

"Attention please! My fellow students, unicorns, and teachers," Darcy said. Madame Shetland looked confused, and Miss Glitterhorn hurried toward the podium to stop Darcy.

"I have an announcement to make!" Darcy continued. "I would like to volunteer as Chief Organizer of the School Dance Committee. Together, we can make this a super-sensational school dance!"

The students burst into applause, as Miss Glitterhorn made it to the podium. "Er, is there a Dance Committee?" Miss Glitterhorn asked Madame Shetland, who shrugged.

"No . . . ," she said thoughtfully, "but why not? Might make things easier for us teachers. That's enough now, Darcy, no need to make everyone do the wave."

"Shall I just do a stage dive and crowd-surf to finish?" Darcy asked the head teacher.

"No, thank you, Darcy." Madame Shetland paused

for a moment to think. "Each class shall look after one part of the dance preparations. Darcy, you may oversee all the arrangements."

As the morning bell rang for lessons, Mira led Dave out of the hall to their classroom and gave him a massive hug. It was so wonderful that Darcy was going to be Chief Organizer of the school dance . . . even if it was a job she'd just made up!

∪∪∪

Darcy didn't waste any time. At morning break, she gathered the first meeting of the Super-Sensational School Dance Committee in the gym. Madame Shetland and Miss Glitterhorn had decided that Class Red would select the music and be in charge of the lighting, and Darcy had decided she would create a super-awesome first dance to get the party started!

Mira and Dave were rushing to the meeting because they were a little late—they'd had to stop for snacks on the way. They passed Jake and his unicorn, Pegasus, doing some cool break-dancing moves down the hallway.

"Let's try that, Dave," Mira said, attempting a wiggle that started in her head and went down to her feet.

Dave watched her, and then did a massive burp. "We can work on your moves," Mira said, pushing the door open.

Inside the gym, Darcy and Star had pushed all the crash mats and benches to the side except for one piece of gym equipment, which Darcy sat behind like it was a desk. Rainbow-colored climbing ropes hung from the ceiling behind her like a curtain. Star counted the children and unicorns coming into the gym and showed them where to sit.

Darcy banged on her makeshift table and

23

signaled for quiet. Freya whispered, "Where did she get the hammer?"

"It's called a gavel," said Raheem.

Mia realized that Darcy was taking the role of Chief Organizer *very* seriously.

"Order, order!" called Darcy. "I declare the first meeting of the Super-Sensational School Dance Committee open!" She paused. "You may applaud."

Everyone quickly started clapping.

"You're welcome," Darcy continued. "The first thing we have to do is—yes, Jake?"

Jake was standing up with his hand raised. "How come YOU'RE committee leader? I think we should have a vote on who should be in charge."

Everyone groaned. Jake ALWAYS wanted to be leader!

"Sit down, Jake. This isn't a quest," called Freya.

Jake went red and started to talk back, but

Darcy just spoke over him. "As I was saying!

The first order of business is . . . the theme for

the dance. Star—are you taking minutes?"

Star blushed and trotted back to Darcy. She took out a notepad and a sparkly gel pen.

Zara from Class Indigo put up her hand. "What about Unicorns from History as a theme?" she said.

"That's fun!" said Mira. "Ooh! Or what about Fireworks? Or Cats?"

"Those are . . . ideas," said Darcy. "*I* was thinking—Star, drumroll, please—Glitter Fever!" Darcy flung her arms out in a big "ta-da" move.

"What about Under the Sea?" said Seb.

Then children started shouting out their ideas all at once:

"Stars!"

"Space!"

"SLOTHS!" Everyone turned to Flo, Freya's

twin sister, and she shrugged. "What? I like sloths."

Darcy shook her head. "Stop just saying things that begin with *S*!" She tried to continue but was interrupted by more theme ideas.

"Unicycles!"

"Umbrellas!"

"Uranium!"

Darcy banged her gavel and looked angry. "Now you're just saying things that begin with *U*. STOP IT! We're having a vote!"

Everyone sat back down, and Darcy smiled. Mira thought it looked a little forced. Darcy continued, "Okay, we'll have a vote on the top three ideas. Everybody close your eyes and raise your hand or hoof for the theme

you like best. Star will count the votes. Close
your eyes now!"

Darcy called out the three theme ideas in
order: Space, Umbrellas, and Glitter Fever. Mira
frowned as she realized that Darcy had decided
which three ideas were the best.

"Do you think she's taking this a bit too
seriously?" Mira whispered to Raheem, opening
one eye.

Raheem shrugged and kept his eyes tightly
shut.

"Keep those hands up, please!" said Darcy
sternly.

Mira thought Star was taking a long time
to count the votes. She realized that Star was

frantically crossing things out on her notepad, then looking up to count the raised hands and hooves again. Mira felt bad for the unicorn. She found counting hard, too, especially under pressure. Sometimes Mira skipped right from twenty-nine to forty if she wasn't thinking carefully.

Dave grunted and shuffled out of the line. Mira guessed he was hungry.

Darcy banged her gavel again and told everyone to open their eyes. Mira could see Dave sniffing around near Darcy. *He's probably searching for snacks*, thought Mira.

"I am thrilled to announce," said Darcy, "that the winner by LOTS of votes is . . . GLITTER FEVER!"

Raheem and Mira clapped, and a few other
students joined in, too. No one looked quite as
excited as Darcy. Freya whispered to Mira,
"That was totally fixed. Darcy just made up
the result."

Mira frowned. She did agree with Freya that
the vote didn't quite seem fair . . . but she knew
Darcy just wanted every part of the dance to be
perfect, and she certainly had lots of great
ideas!

Just then, there was a huge crash behind Darcy.
Raheem screamed and hid behind his chair, and
the other students and unicorns started running
around in a panic. When the dust settled, Mira
saw Dave, thoughtfully chewing the red climbing

rope, with the other ropes in a heap all over Darcy's desk. Darcy sat angrily amid the rubble, covered in dust.

Mira ran over to see if her friend was okay.

Darcy was bright red in the face and did not look happy.

"Darcy, I'm so sorry!" Mira said. "I think Dave thought the red climbing rope was a giant strawberry licorice."

"It's fine!" said Darcy, coughing up some dust. Star trotted around, picking up her notes, which had fallen all over the floor.

Mira kept asking if Darcy was okay as they cleaned up, and Darcy kept saying she was fine, but Mira was sure she heard Darcy muttering "nightmare unicorn" and "super greedy."

The bell rang to end morning break, and

Darcy and Star left the gym quickly, with Darcy still muttering under her breath.

Dave nudged Mira's elbow. She pulled out a real strawberry candy from her pocket for him, and he gave a happy fart in return.

CHAPTER THREE
Glitter Fever . . .

Later that day, after lunch, it was time for PE.

Miss Hind, the PE teacher, blew her whistle and called Class Red together. Mira headed to the back of the group, tugging Dave along with her.

"Now, Class Red, we have a change of lesson plan today," barked Miss Hind. "As you know, Class Red will be opening the school dance with a special routine, which Darcy has created. I am thrilled to be helping you learn your special dance." (Mira couldn't help thinking that Miss Hind didn't look very thrilled.)

Miss Hind pressed play on the speaker. "Here is the song you will be dancing to, written by none other than . . . Darcy. It's called 'Glitter Fever's Gonna Get You.'"

The room suddenly filled with very loud music. Raheem clamped his hands over his ears and squeezed his eyes shut. Darcy whooped and started spinning around in circles in her wheelchair, rainbow wheel rims flashing as she sang along. Flo and her unicorn ran around and around the hall. Even Dave woke up from his nap and flicked his ears back and forth to the music as it filled the air.

Mira felt a little thrill as she tapped her feet.

Disco dancing

Unicorns prancing

Hooves in the air

Like you just don't care

Stable strutting

Popping and tutting

Everybody get down

Glitter fever is coming to town!

Mira couldn't believe Darcy had written a whole song! She felt really proud of her friend, and she couldn't wait to learn the dance routine.

On Mira's very first trip to Unicorn School,

Dave had surprised her by being terrific at prancing. Maybe, just maybe, Dave would also be great at dancing. Maybe they'd get a medal at the dance! After all, dancing was a bit like prancing, but to music . . .

Raheem nudged Mira with his elbow and whispered, "What's . . . glitter fever?"

"What?" Mira whispered back.

"In the song—glitter fever. What is it?" Raheem looked even more worried than usual.

Darcy overheard and jumped in. "Nobody knows, Raheem." She flicked her hair. "But it's going to get you and everyone else!"

"That's what I'm worried about," Raheem replied.

"Mira and Raheem!" shouted Miss Hind. "Stop chatting and get in line with your unicorns."

The children and unicorns were soon standing in two lines, one behind the other. Miss Hind started teaching the dance. "Okay, *five, six, seven, eight*, and children take two steps to the right, unicorns two steps left, turn and look at your partner—snap! Two steps the other way, turn and—snap! And then, children, turn to face your unicorns, hold hands and hooves, and sliiiiiiide . . ."

Star gave a snort as Dave stepped on her hoof.

Pegasus glared as Dave spun around on his belly in a circle, making Mira laugh loudly.

"Come *on*, Dave!" snapped Darcy. "That's not one of the dance moves!"

Mira frowned. "It's Dave's first time, Darcy. We'll get it in the end. Not all the unicorns can do different things with their front and back legs."

Miss Hind called Darcy and Star up to the front to demonstrate the next move.

The next move was actually a long series of moves. They all tried to follow Darcy and Star, but it was a struggle. Two unicorns fell over.

"It's very complicated," said Mira, poking herself in the eye.

"Don't worry, it's just armography," said Darcy.

Jake and his unicorn, Pegasus, got the hang of it right away, and looked really cool. Freya got the giggles when she accidentally hit herself in the nose. Flo and her unicorn, Sparkles, looked like they might cry because they couldn't do it. Raheem and Brave just looked lost.

Dave really was trying hard to get it right. But as he and Mira tried the moves, his legs got tangled and, very slowly, he toppled over and caused all the other unicorns to tumble down.

Darcy glared at them all. "Seriously! Stop messing around!"

"We're not messing around!" Mira shouted back.

Freya put her hands on her hips. "Darcy, none of us have ever done this before. You and Star were rehearsing all through lunchtime, so you've got a head start."

"Some of us are just naturally talented, actually!" said Darcy, as Star's stomach rumbled. She looked embarrassed and hid behind Darcy's wheelchair.

Miss Hind blew her whistle. "That's enough dancing for now, class. Let's move on to ab work."

"Ab . . . a-a-ab work?" stammered Raheem.

"Yes," said Miss Hind. "A strong core is essential for a dancer's posture."

CHAPTER FOUR
Quest Countdown

At dinnertime, when Mira and Dave sat down at the dinner table, Star had her muzzle on the table and was snoring. Dave gave her a nudge. She woke up with a snort.

"Is she okay?" asked Freya through a mouthful of mashed potato.

"She's fine," said Darcy. "Star, we have lots to do. Don't get lazy like Dave."

"Darcy! That's not nice," said Raheem.

Dave did not seem to be offended. Very calmly, he took a big bite out of Darcy's clipboard.

"Mira!" Darcy shrieked. "Those are my super-important party-planning notes. Make him STOP!"

Seb arrived and plonked his dinner tray down in between Darcy and Dave. "Can I draw some posters for the dance? Firework and I had some ideas for the Glitter Fever theme."

Darcy wiped Dave's slobber off the clipboard

with her sleeve. "That sounds great, Seb. Thank you. Star and I have already started working on some designs . . . but perhaps you can color them in?"

Mira frowned. Why was Darcy speaking so weirdly . . . like a teacher or a parent?

"Ooh, ooh!" Flo put up her hand. "Can Sparkles and I be on the Welcoming Committee? We thought it would be lovely to sprinkle glitter confetti over people as they walk into the dance."

"Hmm, that might be nice," said Darcy thoughtfully. "I mean, it's supposed to be Class Yellow's job, but I'm sure we can help them. As long as the glitter confetti is gold and matches the rest of the color scheme."

"Pegasus and I can be in charge of the food," said Jake. "We like baking."

Darcy smiled. "Happy for you to help. Just make sure you follow the recipes carefully. Star, are you taking notes on all this?"

Mira narrowed her eyes. Darcy was becoming dance obsessed, and she didn't even sound like herself anymore. What was going on?

The next morning, the first lesson was science. Miss Glitterhorn clapped to start the class, just as Jake and Pegasus jogged in.

"Sorry, miss, we were doing some extra training for the quest this afternoon," said Jake, panting.

Mira smiled to herself. The thought of the quest made her stomach flutter. Quests were Mira's absolute favorite thing!

Darcy raised her hand. "Speaking of the quest, Miss Glitterhorn, don't you think Class Red is too young for such an important task? I mean, maybe we should all stay behind and work on the dance?"

"Can we have one lesson that's NOT about the dance?" Mira said, frowning at Darcy. "That's all you're interested in at the moment!"

Miss Glitterhorn glared at the two of them. "Now, now, girls. Class Red is perfect for this quest. We need to collect Warming Crystals before winter comes to the land. Warming Crystals form in small, honeycomb pockets in the walls of the Crystal Maze Mine. Since you're the youngest and smallest, your hands are the perfect size to fit into the holes and collect the crystals."

Miss Glitterhorn drew a series of diagrams on the whiteboard, demonstrating how the crystals should be carefully removed from the cavern wall, with each human and unicorn pair working together to release the crystal. Everyone took notes, apart from Dave, who was noisily eating chips, and Darcy, who was listening to music and sketching party outfits in her notebook.

"Now!" their teacher continued. "Today we are also learning about the reflective properties of glitter and crystals! One person from each

pair, please come up to collect the mirrors and flashlights."

Darcy and Mira were *supposed* to be working together. But Darcy just kept whispering to Star and making her write down things about the dance. So Mira had to go up and get their mirrors and flashlights.

Miss Glitterhorn explained how light bounced off shiny surfaces and made things sparkle. Flo was sticking little squares of mirror to Sparkles's horn to make it shine like a crystal. Dave thought that was funny and spiked a mirror tile on the end of his horn. As he turned to show Mira, the morning sunlight caught on the mirror and shined directly into Darcy's eyes.

"Argh!" she yelled. "Dave! I can't see anyth—
OH! I've had a BRILLIANT IDEA!"

Miss Glitterhorn clapped in delight. "About
reflection?"

"No, well, sort of . . ." Darcy stopped herself.
"Um, when is the quest again?"

"After lunch, Darcy. Now, what was your
brilliant idea?"

"Oh, nothing. I forgot." Darcy smiled a
small and very secret smile. As Mira helped
Dave get the mirror off his horn, she
wondered what Darcy was up to. She was
sure it had something to do with the
dance . . .

After lunch, it was time for the quest! Not only were quests Mira's favorite thing about Unicorn School BUT there was always the chance of getting a medal. Mira was so excited that she was hopping from foot to foot. Dave started hopping, too, then stepped on Mira's toe.

Class Red lined up outside the unicorn stables. Colin the caretaker was handing out coveralls and helmets with headlamps for Class Red students and hornlamps for the unicorns. The children changed into their safety gear and helped glitter-shoe their unicorns. Glitter helped to protect the unicorns, and they *always* put glitter on their hooves before a quest.

Raheem asked Colin if the unicorns needed

helmets, too, for safety. Colin said no, unicorn skulls were much stronger than children's, and they were so hard they could probably even win a headbutting contest with a rhinoceros. Raheem looked a bit pale and asked if it was likely they might see a rhinoceros in the mine. Colin said no and kept checking that everyone's unicorns had been glitter-shoed.

Miss Hind blew her whistle and glared at the class. "Okay! Everyone please mount your unicorns and follow me. I want a nice, clean quest with no funny business or you can FORGET about going to the school dance. Oh, and I've decided that your quest leader will be Jake."

Jake's "YES!" was so loud that Sparkles cantered

off in fright. Flo went to fetch her, and a few

minutes later, they all set off into the forest.

Raheem had insisted that Brave wear a helmet,

even though he did NOT look happy about it.

But finally they were on their quest! Mira didn't even mind that Jake was quest leader. She threw Dave a doughnut and he happily trotted after it, giving Mira a little butt wiggle to say thanks.

Maybe, just this once, Mira would get to have a normal, completely amazing quest. She couldn't wait to get started!

CHAPTER FIVE
The Crystal Maze Mine

The entrance to the Crystal Maze Mine was in a rough, gray cliff edge at the other side of the Fearsome Forest. Mira was surprised to see a railway track in front of the mine.

"We're getting a TRAIN?" said Raheem, his eyes wide. "I thought it was just a cave! How deep underground is it?"

"We're going to the center of the earth!" sang Flo as she trotted past with Sparkles.

"The center of the earth?" repeated Raheem, his eyes widening. "What if we never get out?!"

Miss Hind blew her whistle as Mira comforted
Raheem. "Okay, Class Red, please come and get
one special collection box each. These are *very*
high-tech and very precious. You will each fill all
six spaces with a Warming Crystal, and no more!
We need this exact number of Warming Crystals
to heat the school and unicorns through the
winter. We must only collect what we truly
need, no more and nothing else. Remember
Unicorn School Rule 73: Leave the Forest as You
Find It."

Jake helped hand out the special collection
boxes, which had six little holes and a lid.

"Are these . . . egg cartons?" asked Seb. "I
thought you said they were high-tech."

58

"No talking back!" shouted Miss Hind. "Yes, they were inspired by egg cartons—a perfect piece of design. Now, you will each get into the railway carts, children in front to steer, unicorns in the back. Keep all arms, legs, and unicorns inside the cart at all times! The way to the Warming Crystal Cavern is VERY WELL SIGNPOSTED. Do not go off the rickety railway tracks, and DO NOT GO anywhere other than the Warming Crystal Cavern. Go straight there and come straight back once you have filled your egg cartons. I mean, special collection boxes. Understood?"

"Understood!" Class Red shouted back at Miss Hind.

"Why is it called the *rickety* railway track?" whispered Raheem.

Before anyone had time to answer, the class raced to the railway carts, fighting to get into the front carts.

"Remember, children, please sit in the front of the railway carts. Jake will be driving in the front cart and steering, and all the carts are attached to

each other, so everyone else should be able to sit
back and enjoy the ride."

Raheem buckled himself and Brave into their
cart, looking pretty queasy. Mira jumped in the

cart next to his and lured Dave into the back
with a piece of chocolate.

Miss Hind told them all to switch on their
headlamps and waved them off into the mine.
As Mira was near the back, she could see Miss Hind
watching a unicorn wrestling match on her phone
even before the train was completely in the tunnel.

Everything went dark. Raheem whimpered
a little. Mira did think this quest seemed a little
dangerous. It was so exciting!

Jake started leading a teamwork song:

"1, 2, 3, 4, together we achieve much more!
5, 6, 7, 8, unicorns are really great!"

Mira joined in, and smiled when she could hear Darcy singing the loudest of all. Darcy loved singing.

Dave was scratching at his hornlamp with a front hoof. The light flickered on and off, bouncing against the tunnel walls. Brave hiccupped.

"Dave, can you stop that?" asked Raheem.

Mira turned around. "I think his hornlamp is really uncomfortable," she said.

"It's making Brave trainsick."

Brave hiccupped again.

Mira fed Dave another treat to stop him from fidgeting. Thanks to the light coming from the headlights and hornlights, Mira could see that there were lots of tunnels and railway tracks

leading off from their tunnel. As they trundled down the track, they saw little bits of crystals and precious gemstones all around, glinting in the walls and the ceiling. They passed a sign for the Emerald Cave, and Mira saw an incredible green glow from the tunnel.

"Raheem, I think we're nearly at the Glitter Slime Gorge!" Mira said eagerly.

Raheem just gulped, but there were "oohs"

from the rest of the class as they caught sight
of the spectacularly sparkly cliff edge through
an opening in the wall.

There was a huge SLURP sound, and a glitter boulder popped out from the top of the gorge, slipping down the cliff with a trail of oozing, sparkly slime. Mira thought she saw someone lean out of a cart up ahead, and Raheem yelped, "SAFETY FIRST! Stay inside the carts!"

The railway carts turned another corner and down a small slope and then stopped. Jake—who was clutching a map of the Crystal Maze Mine—announced that they had arrived at the Warming Crystal Cavern.

The unicorns and their humans climbed out of the tunnel (Dave had fallen asleep during the journey, and Flo had to help Mira lift him out of the cart, still snoring loudly). It got warmer as

they left the tunnel and turned into the cavern.
It was quite dark, and Mira was glad she was
wearing her headlamp. Other pairs had already
started collecting crystals, so Mira woke
Dave and hurried to find an empty section
of wall.

Mira remembered from science class how
to feel along the wall for a soft section, then get
Dave to poke a hole in the crystal crust with
his horn. She scooped out dirt from the hole
and reached in until her fingers felt something
smooth and round. With a bit more digging,
she just about got her fingers around the crystal.
It felt warm in her hand. Gently, she pulled it out
and gasped. In response, Dave gave a huge belch.

The Warming Crystal was the size of a large marble, and it started to swirl all kinds of beautiful colors, from green to blue to purple, just like the amazing rainbow lights from the last quest Mira had been on.

She carefully popped the crystal into the special collection box.

Mira worked quickly to fill her box with more crystals and gave Dave a little hug. This was fun! Someone started to sing the teamwork song again and Mira joined in, but she realized it sounded quieter than before. Something was missing . . .

Mira looked around the cavern. Then she realized it wasn't some*thing* that was missing; it was some*one*. Darcy had disappeared!

CHAPTER SIX
Glitter Slime Gorge

Mira panicked. Where could Darcy *be*?

She thought fast. Dragging Dave behind her, she scuttled over to Raheem and Brave.

"Raheem," she hissed. "Darcy's missing!"

Raheem looked around. "Uh-oh," he said. "And her railway cart's gone, too."

"Come on! We've got to go find her. She could be in trouble!"

Raheem looked scared. "But . . . but we're not supposed to leave this cavern!"

"Raheem, we HAVE to find Darcy!" said

Mira firmly. "She could be ANYWHERE. And she's our friend. We have to find her and bring her back safely."

Raheem sighed nervously. "Okay, fine, but shouldn't we at least tell Jake where we're going?"

"NO! We've got to do this secretly. Follow me," whispered Mira.

They snuck off to the last railway cart and put their egg cartons full of Warming Crystals carefully inside. Luckily, the other students and unicorns were distracted by gathering the crystals. Mira unhooked the cart from the one in front of it and put her last doughnut on the edge of the cart. Dave shunted forward to gobble it up and set the cart trundling off down

the railway track. Mira pushed Raheem and the
two unicorns inside while it was moving, and
then jumped in.

"How . . . how do you know which way we're
going?" Raheem asked in a trembly voice.

"I don't," said Mira.

"What?!"

"I figured you would have memorized the map," Mira said.

"Oh, right," said Raheem. "Yes, I have. So, where do you want to look first?"

They decided to retrace their steps.

They poked their heads into the Glorious Opal Shaft, but Darcy wasn't there. Then they checked in the Emerald Cave, but there was no sign of her there, either. Back in the main tunnel, two large glittery boulders rolled past them. They shivered. Then Mira remembered Darcy's love of glitter . . . After all, she had chosen the dance theme Glitter Fever AND written the song "Glitter Fever's

Gonna Get You." Suddenly Mira knew JUST where Darcy would be. "The Glitter Slime Gorge!" she shrieked, making Raheem jump.

Raheem directed Mira back to the cliff, and then reached over suddenly to pull the brake. Everyone jerked forward, and Brave groaned. Dave, on the other hand, was whinnying joyfully. He seemed to really like the railway when he could stay awake.

Raheem pointed straight ahead. Mira looked at the track, which sloped into a steep, steep spiral to the bottom of the Glitter Slime Gorge.

"Maybe she's not—" began Raheem, just as they heard someone singing "Glitter Fever's Gonna Get You" at the bottom of the cliff.

"If that's not Darcy, then Dave's not my unicorn," said Mira, and flipped off the brake, sending them whizzing down the track like a roller coaster.

"**W**we**EEE**ee**EE**," cried Mira.

"**AAA**rrggg**HH**," shrieked

Raheem.

"**BLE**eeug**HH**," groaned Brave.

"**BBR**rrrrr**RRRR**," snorted Dave

happily, his muzzle hanging over the side of the

railway cart, tongue waggling in the rush of air.

THUMP!

They came to a sudden stop by bumping

into another cart at the bottom of the gorge.

They all shivered. It really was chilly down

here.

"Hooves in the air, like you just don't care! Glitter fever is comin' to town!"

Raheem and Mira clambered out of the cart and turned a corner to see Darcy riding Star, singing happily and clutching two giant Sticky Glitter boulders. Her eyes had a wild look in them. Star was rolling a couple more glitter boulders along the ground toward the carts with her hooves.

"She looks a bit . . . strange," Mira whispered to Raheem.

Raheem nodded wisely. "She's got glitter fever."

Mira thought for a moment and then turned sideways and held out her hands in front of her, fingers spread. She edged toward Darcy, who

was still singing very loudly and didn't seem to have noticed them.

"What are you doing?" asked Raheem.

"I saw this on a TV show about bears," replied Mira. "When they're worked up, you have to approach with great caution."

Then she said in a soothing voice, "Darcy, it's okay, you're not going to be in trouble, just put down the glitter boulders and come back with us."

"NO!" said Darcy with wide eyes and a huge smile. "Can't you see? Sticky Glitter boulders are just what the dance needs! These Sticky Glitter boulders will make the most amazing disco balls. We'll hang them up and shine lights on them, and it will be EPIC! Woohoo!"

Star whinnied in agreement.

"Mira's right, Darcy," said Raheem. "We're not supposed to be here, and we're not supposed to take anything other than the Warming Crystals out of the mine. Remember School Rule 73: Leave the Forest as You Find It?"

"Yes, Raheem. Firstly, we are not technically *in* the forest. And secondly, Miss Hind said 'only take what you need.' And we NEED these glitter boulders!" Star was now nudging the boulders toward the train tracks and trying to roll them up into the cart.

"Darcy, NO!" Mira gave up using her soothing voice. Darcy was being totally selfish! "We'll ALL get into so much trouble! Leave the Sticky Glitter boulders here and let's just get back to the quest." Mira rolled Star's boulders away from the tracks.

"GIVE THOSE BACK!" shouted Darcy. "The school dance needs them!"

"No, we NEED to get back to the quest! The

dance really doesn't matter THAT much," Mira
yelled back.

"It DOES matter!" Darcy kept tight hold of
the Sticky Glitter boulders. "Raheem, you can
tell Mira that I'm no longer speaking to her."

Mira crossed her arms and turned to Raheem.
"You can tell Darcy that *I'm* not speaking to *her*."

"Well, you can tell Mira that I wouldn't have
to stop speaking to her if her unicorn hadn't
destroyed my meeting AND eaten my committee
notes!"

Mira glared at Darcy. "Well, you can tell Darcy
that if she wasn't being so incredibly annoying
about the dance, maybe Dave wouldn't have felt
the need to EAT HER NOTES!"

As Mira and Darcy kept yelling at each other, Raheem looked back and forth at his friends, his head moving from side to side.

"STOP YELLING!" he finally shouted, accidentally knocking one of the Sticky Glitter boulders out of Darcy's hands so that it splattered on the floor in an oozy lump of slime.

CHAPTER SEVEN
To the Rescue!

Looking a bit shocked, Darcy let the other Sticky Glitter boulder roll down onto the floor. She wiped her nose on her sleeve.

"Look," she said, sniffing, "I'm not the best at anything at Unicorn School. Raheem, you're so smart, and Mira, you always manage to get medals despite Dave being, you know, different. But I LOVE dancing, and I just wanted to show everyone what a good job I could do with the school dance. Maybe I did get a bit carried away."

Mira suddenly felt sorry for her friend. "Darcy, you're doing an amazing job. You're a great committee leader! But if we don't get back to the group soon, Miss Hind will find out you went missing, and then *no one* will get to enjoy the dance." Mira paused for a moment and looked at Darcy's sad face. "Listen, I know we're not allowed to take anything from the mine, but this Sticky Glitter really is awesome. Maybe you could just take back a few bits that have already broken off?"

Darcy nodded hard. "I mean," she said, "when you think about it, we're really just rescuing it!" She turned to Dave. "Dave, I'm sorry I snapped at you. I didn't mean it!"

Dave, who was rummaging around in the back of the cart, turned and shrugged.

"Can we please just get a move on and head back to the rest of the class?" asked Raheem. He was jiggling nervously from foot to foot.

Darcy and Mira agreed, and they quickly got back in the carts.

No one moved.

"Uh-oh," said Raheem, his eyes widening.

"What?" Darcy and Mira replied at the same time.

"We're stuck at the bottom of a steep hill," Raheem shrieked. "We can't get back up the rickety railway spiral!"

"There must be a way. We've just got to think positive," said Darcy.

86

Raheem tried his deep, calming breaths.

"No, we've got the two rear railway carts.

The front cart is the only one with an engine. We might be stuck down here forever!"

Brave gave Raheem a hug. Dave gave a sympathetic fart. A colorful cloud appeared behind him. It smelled of marshmallows.

Mira looked at Dave. Had he just farted out a *rainbow cloud*? She shook her head. That was pretty strange, but right now she had bigger things to worry about. She *really* didn't want to be stuck in the Glitter Slime Gorge forever!

Dave farted loudly again, and this time the cloud was pink. Mira heard a crunching sound. She looked at Dave, then at her egg carton. Two crystals were missing. She narrowed her eyes. "Dave! Did you eat the Warming Crystals?"

Dave stopped chewing, then let out another noisy fart cloud, a massive one this time. The cart shot forward a little way, and he jumped in surprise at its power.

"Dave, eating the crystals is genuinely a very bad thing to do!" said Darcy admiringly.

"Dave, you're actually a genius!" said Mira. "Quick, finish the crystals." Before her friends could object, she fed Dave the rest of the egg carton and shoved his butt over the back edge of the cart.

Dave gobbled up the crystals, swallowed, and licked his lips.

Then, with an almighty blast and an extra-large cloud, Dave did an enormous rainbow fart and—

WHOOOSH!—the railway carts launched back up the train tracks.

"WHEEEEEEEEE!" yelled Darcy, with her hands in the air.

"**AAAAAAAARGH!**" cried Raheem.
"**WOOOHOOOO!**" shrieked Mira.

Even Raheem was giddy with excitement by the time they turned the last spiral corner and got back up to the main tunnel. He guided the carts down the tracks to the Warming Crystal Cavern. Mira couldn't believe they'd made it. They'd rescued Darcy *and* made it safely back to the group. Maybe no one had even noticed they were gone. They could just fill their egg cartons quickly. And then finish the quest!

"Where have you BEEN?" Jake yelled at them as soon as they crept into the Warming Crystal Cavern. His face was a funny color and he looked really worried.

"I told you they'd come back," said Freya. "It's
cool, come on. Time to go."

"You're going to be in SO MUCH
TROUBLE," said Jake threateningly.

Seb put a hand on his shoulder. "Jake, it's

fine. They're here now. Let's just get back to Miss Hind."

Jake held up their empty egg cartons from the railway cart. "It's NOT fine—their special collection boxes are empty! We need to fill every single one. I'm quest leader, remember? I know this stuff!" Jake was really red in the face now.

Darcy rolled her eyes. "Jake, don't be so dramatic. Let's just hurry up, fill our egg boxes, and get back in the carts."

Jake scowled and told everyone else to start loading up the railway carts.

Mira, Darcy, and Raheem headed to an empty cave wall section.

"Thanks, Jake!" said Mira brightly, as she started

feeling for a Warming Crystal pocket in the wall. "Darcy, here's one!"

Mira and Darcy grinned at each other. It felt SO good for everything to be back to normal! Jake rolled his eyes and yelled, "Just HURRY UP!" then stormed off to boss around the children and unicorns getting back into the railway carts.

∪ ∪ ∪

The return journey was very happy. Even Jake cheered up as he led everyone in a loud rendition of the teamwork song. At last they saw a little bit of sunlight at the end of the tunnel and soon were out in the forest again.

Miss Hind counted the children as they got out

of the carts. "Seventeen, Raheem . . . eighteen, Darcy—WHAT IS THAT?!"

"What is what, Miss Hind?" said Darcy innocently.

"The glittery thing poking out of your backpack," said Miss Hind.

Darcy gasped, opening her bag. "A glitter boulder!" she said. "Oh no! It must have accidentally fallen into my bag."

Miss Hind narrowed her eyes.

"I mean, I guess it'll look super cool at the dance, so it's lucky, really . . . ," Darcy carried on.

Miss Hind loomed over Darcy. "That's not a disco ball, Darcy—it's Sticky Glitter from the Glitter Slime Gorge. You should not have been

anywhere near that gorge! The quest was very clear, Darcy: *only* collect the Warming Crystals and come straight back. School Rule 73: Leave the Forest as You Find It."

A crowd of their classmates had gathered to see what all the fuss was about, and everyone started oohing and aahing at the Sticky Glitter.

Miss Hind looked like she might explode. She picked up the Sticky Glitter and hurled it back into the tunnel. It took her a couple of tries, because the glitter was sticking to her hands. It really was very sticky. She turned back to the class. Her face had turned a strange shade of purple.

"Class Red, you disobeyed my instructions and

MUST be punished. Therefore, none of you will go to the school dance!" shouted Miss Hind.

The whole class gasped.

"B-But, Miss Hind," stammered Darcy, "it was my—"

"SILENCE!" yelled Miss Hind. "If I hear one more word from any of you, then you'll all be in even MORE trouble!"

CHAPTER EIGHT
Disco Disaster

The journey back through the Fearsome Forest was very quiet. Mira had run out of snacks, so Dave kept veering off the path to try to eat the sparklebushes. Soon they were way behind the rest of the class.

Mira sighed. "Oh, Dave, I was so looking forward to the dance." Dave snorted in sympathy. "And I was so excited about the quest! But now we don't get to dance together, or win any medals."

Dave turned his head to try to cheer her up

but accidentally tossed Mira into a bush. He licked her face to apologize.

Mira was brushing leaves off her sweater when she heard someone giggling and saw Flo waiting on the path.

"What's so funny?" Mira asked.

"Oh, I'm just happy," said Flo. "I know we can't go to the dance, but wasn't the quest fun? And my coveralls are so pretty! I'm NEVER going to take them off. And I'm spending time with my BEST friend." Flo gave Sparkles a big hug.

Mira smiled and hauled herself back up onto Dave. They trotted down the path together. Flo was right. They had done the right thing by rescuing Darcy, even though it meant they all

couldn't go to the dance. As Dave let out a small,
colorful fart cloud, Mira couldn't help but smile.
Whatever else happened, she still had her UBFF!

∪ ∪ ∪

Back at the stables, everyone took off their
coveralls and put them in a big laundry basket
(everyone apart from Flo, who smuggled hers
back to her room). They led their unicorns into
their stalls and groomed them, mane to tail. Mira
gave Dave fresh hay in his feed bag and fresh
straw for his bed.

Behind her, Mira heard Jake boasting to some
of their classmates.

"I can't believe I collected SO MANY crystals.
There were actually too many for the boxes, so I
had to leave most of them behind. One of them
was SO HOT it nearly burned my arm off. I
basically aced the quest, before Darcy ruined it
for everyone."

A few of the children sighed and looked sad. Mira wanted to stick up for Darcy, but she could see how disappointed they all were about missing out on the dance.

Mira saw that Dave already finished his hay, so she went out to get him some more and bumped into Seb coming out of Star's stable.

"Have you seen Darcy?" Seb asked.

"No, why?" said Mira.

"She's missing again. So is Star."

Mira felt hot, and her heart started racing. Darcy had been very quiet the entire way home. She obviously felt really bad about making the whole class miss the dance.

Maybe Darcy had run away with Star into the

forest . . . or maybe she'd gone into hiding . . . or maybe she had gone back home early through the Magic Portal and they'd never see her again? Mira had only just made up with her best friend. What if she'd lost her again, for good?!

Just then, Mira heard a familiar clap and turned to see Miss Glitterhorn in the stable yard, standing next to Miss Hind, Darcy, and Star.

"You didn't run away to live in the forest!" Mira shouted, and flung herself at Darcy.

"Uh, thank you, Mira," said Miss Glitterhorn, and she clapped her hands again. "Class Red, Darcy has something to say to you all."

Darcy pushed Mira off (in a friendly way) and cleared her throat. With a solemn face, she said,

"I'm sorry that I have caused so much trouble. I only wanted everyone to have a completely and utterly amazing school dance. I explained to Miss Glitterhorn that everything was my fault—I took the Sticky Glitter from the caves and I'm the one who disobeyed the quest directions."

Star snorted as if she was apologizing, too.

Darcy looked around at Class Red. "I said to Miss Glitterhorn that I don't think you should all be punished for something I did."

Miss Glitterhorn nodded her head. "Darcy has done the right thing and taken full responsibility for the Sticky Glitter incident. Therefore I am pleased to say that the rest of the class SHALL go to the dance!"

Most of the students cheered loudly, but Mira and Raheem didn't feel like cheering.

Freya ran over to give Darcy a thank-you hug, and soon everyone followed. Even Jake gave Darcy a high five. Then he and Pegasus break-danced back to the stables.

Flo sniffed and wiped her nose on her sleeve. "But it's just so sad you can't come to the dance, too!"

Darcy gave her another hug. "It's fine. You and Sparkles are amazing dancers. You lead the dance for me, okay?"

Once everyone had headed back to the dormitories, talking about what they were going to wear to the dance, Mira and Raheem went to join Darcy. Mira gave her a huge hug. Raheem

shook her hand. "That was a really nice thing you did," he said.

Darcy shrugged, but she had tears in her eyes. "Thanks, you two. Come on, Star, let's get you to bed. We've got a long day of picking up poop tomorrow in detention."

Mira heard Dave give an "I'm hungry" snort from his stable—she'd forgotten to get him his extra hay. "Are you sure you're okay, Darcy? Can I help you groom Star?"

"I'm fine." Darcy sniffed. "Dave needs you. We'll see you in the morning."

Mira went to pick up more hay for Dave and watched Darcy wheel into Star's stable. She felt awful that Darcy couldn't go to the dance.

Even though Darcy *had* caused all the trouble, she'd only done it because she wanted the dance to be the best EVER. Mira just wished there was a way to help Darcy without getting anyone else into trouble . . .

CHAPTER NINE
Friends Together

All lessons were canceled the next morning so that everyone could get ready for the dance in the afternoon. Darcy and Star were very quiet at breakfast before they headed out to the stables for their detention of picking up poop and stable cleaning.

No one was surprised when Jake announced himself the new Chief Organizer of the dance committee for last-minute preparations. But they *were* surprised when he and Pegasus welcomed them all into the hall with a tray of delicious-looking pastries!

"I didn't know Jake was such a terrific baker!" said Mira, scarfing down a large chocolate éclair.

Raheem fed Brave a chocolate croissant. "It turns out Pegasus is half French," he said.

"These are delicious!" cried Mira through a mouthful of pastry. Dave ate five éclairs and gave a happy fart.

Jake gave out party assignments to all the different students. Mira and Dave were sent to mix the fruit punch, then help make the unicorns' party outfits. Jake had even prepared a pile of doughnuts for Dave to snack on so he wouldn't cause too much chaos. Mira had to admit, when Jake channeled all his annoyingness into being in charge, he was actually pretty good at it.

Mira was trying to squeeze Dave into his dancing jacket, but he wouldn't stop wriggling. "Hold still, Dave!" she said. "Do you want another doughnut? Oh, you've already finished them."

Dave snorted and then looked pointedly out the window.

Mira saw where he was looking. Darcy and Star were shoveling unicorn poop in the stable yard.

Mira looked around her. Everywhere she turned, students and unicorns were creating a magical disco room. Sparkly decorations were going up on the walls while twinkly lights crisscrossed the ceiling. And the treats table was looking spectacular. Darcy would love it.

Dave snuffled again and farted loudly.

"Okay, okay!" said Mira, as she took off Dave's dancing jacket. "I agree that Darcy is our friend and the dance won't be nearly as fun without her."

Dave nodded and waggled his ears.

Mira thought for a moment. She thought of dancing in the kitchen with Pickles and Rani. They'd had so much fun, even though it was just the three of them . . . WAIT A MINUTE!

Mira had an idea. But she needed the help of her friends.

Mira quickly whispered in Dave's ear, and Dave trotted over to Brave. He and Raheem were helping to set up the speakers for the DJ.

Brave and Dave started snuffling at each other. Raheem came over to ask Mira what was going on. She explained that the unicorns were going to create a diversion.

Raheem looked both confused and scared.

Just then, Brave gave one of his thundering neighs, and when everyone turned to look at him, Dave kicked over a large speaker. This in turn banged into the treats table, knocking over a unicorn made from cream puffs that

Jake and Pegasus had been creating for several
hours.

Miss Hind, who was overseeing the preparations,
blew her whistle loudly and ran over to see what
was going on, as cream puffs rolled all over the
floor. Mira quickly ducked down and grabbed a
handful of treats from the table and a spare string of
sparkly lights.

Jake went bright red and started stomping around and shouting, and while Miss Hind was calming him down, Mira whispered, "Now's our chance!"

She picked up Darcy's and Star's party outfits from the rail and yanked Raheem out of the hall, with Dave and Brave following closely behind. Mira noticed that Dave had several cream puffs skewered on his horn and was throwing them into the air and catching them in his mouth.

"What now?" asked Raheem, as he stumbled down the hall after Mira.

"We're going to see Darcy," said Mira.

Raheem rolled his eyes and groaned. "Mira, Darcy is in detention and it's all fine, and we're

preparing for the dance, and it's all going to
be nice and calm, with no more danger. Or
excitement."

"No," said Mira, marching them all off toward
the stables. "We owe it to our friend to give her
the very best dance party ever!"

"What are you doing here?" exclaimed Darcy.
She and Star were looking at pictures on Darcy's
phone.

"Darcy, you SHALL go to the dance!" said
Mira dramatically.

Darcy frowned. "I can't go to the dance, Mira.
I'll get in so much trouble!"

Mira grinned. "Aha! Well if Darcy can't come

to the dance, then WE'LL bring the dance to
Darcy!"

"Oh, okay!" said Darcy. She looked confused.
"Actually, I don't understand what's going on."

"We're having our own dance. Just us!" cried
Mira. "And the theme is Glitter Fever."

Darcy blinked in surprise.

"We've brought all the stuff," continued Mira,
giving Darcy a slightly squashed cream puff.
"There's just one thing we need."

"A Chief Organizer," said Raheem, handing
Darcy a clipboard. "The best party planner
ever."

Darcy stared at the clipboard, and then looked
up at them. She frowned. Mira's heart sank.

"You guys . . .," Darcy said slowly, "had better watch out. Because . . ."

Darcy spun around in her chair and pointed her finger at Mira and Raheem. "GLITTER FEVER'S GONNA GET YOU!"

"YAY!" said Mira, and Raheem grinned (but he also pulled his T-shirt up over his mouth, just in case glitter fever *was* something that could make you sick).

Darcy turned back to Mira. "So where *is* our dance?"

"The dorm," Mira said with a great big grin. "But first, we need to make an epic disco ball."

Darcy squealed with delight, and the three friends quickly set about gathering as much

glitter and sparkle as they could find. Darcy had
stashed away the small glitter boulder from earlier,
and Star sorted as much glittery unicorn poop
from their muck pile as possible.

Mira got all the coveralls out of the laundry basket and shook the glitter dust off them. Raheem even went and got all the hand mirrors from the unicorn grooming store.

"Okay, let's make this into a disco ball!" said Mira.

When they'd finished, Darcy wiped her hands on her pants, then wiped a tear from her eye. "It's beautiful," she said. "You are the best friends ever. And this is going to be the best DANCE ever!"

"Even though it's just us," said Raheem.

"*Especially* because it's just us," said Mira, as she gave each of her best friends a big hug.

CHAPTER TEN
Dave Does Disco!

The lunch bell rang, and Mira nodded to her friends. "Quick! Before anyone sees us!" she said.

Dave's stomach rumbled.

"Are you okay?" she asked him. Dave nodded. Today, friendship meant more than anything— even lunch.

They worked as a team. Dave, Star, and Brave rolled the disco ball from the stableyard up into the Class Red dormitory. Mira and Raheem followed them with brooms, sweeping up the glittery, poopy trail they left behind them. Darcy supervised and gave instructions.

They hid the disco ball behind one of the Class Red dorm curtains and ran down to the cafeteria.

"Where did you guys go?" said Jake, as they sat down at the table with their trays. There were smears of chocolate on his face, and he looked a little frazzled.

"Oh, we were just . . . around!" replied Mira, trying to look calm. She was still pretty sweaty and a bit stinky from creating the disco ball. "We were making . . . something. Actually, I really wanted your opinion on a recipe for croissants . . ."

Mira knew that asking Jake for advice would distract him. Soon everyone was chatting about how excited they were for the dance (apart from Jake, who was still going on about croissants).

The lunch bell rang again and there was a stampede of students and unicorns running to the dance. Whoops and cheers came from the hall, and then music started blaring out.

"Are you sure you don't mind missing it?" asked Darcy quietly.

Mira gave her a huge hug. "Are you kidding?" she said cheerfully. "Let's go and have our own dorm disco!"

∪ ∪ ∪

Back in the Class Red dormitory, Raheem put on some music and moved all the bedside lamps to shine on the disco ball. He put the disco ball

on a record player on a bedside table so it would spin and send sparkly light all over the walls. They all got changed into their party outfits, and Darcy had the idea of taking down one of the red curtains to make a red carpet. Then they took turns pretending to arrive in style with their unicorns.

They were dancing around and singing at the top of their voices and didn't hear the door bang. So they were quite surprised when they did hear the

SSrreeeeeCHHH

of Miss Hind's whistle.

"WHAT are you DOING in here?!" the PE teacher yelled at them.

Mira noticed that Miss Hind wasn't wearing her usual sportswear. Instead she was wearing a white, shiny party dress, and she'd even styled her hair in a swishy ponytail instead of a scraped-back bun.

"You look lovely, Miss Hind!" said Darcy.

Raheem sank down on the bed, his head in his hands. "I knew it! We're in even more trouble. We'll be banned from Unicorn School forever. Expelled! Sent to prison!"

Miss Hind pointed at them all in turn. "Darcy, YOU should be in detention. Mira, YOU should be at the dance, and Raheem, YOU should be in the lighting booth, and—WHAT IS THAT BEAUTIFUL THING?!"

The three friends followed Miss Hind's finger, which was now pointing at their disco ball.

Darcy stepped in to defend her friends. "It's a disco ball, Miss Hind. Again, this is all my fault. Mira and Raheem didn't want me to feel left out, so they made me a dance party in the dorm. Please, let them go back to the dance. I'll go back to detention. I'm sorry!"

Mira was shocked to hear Darcy saying it was her fault, when the dorm disco had been Mira's idea! She started to explain that to Miss Hind, but the teacher's face was now doing funny things. Her eyebrows looked angry, her cheeks were bright red, and her mouth was trying really hard not to smile.

"Grrrr," Miss Hind growled. "This is all extremely frustrating. Although NONE of you

are where you should be, you have behaved in a way that promotes the Unicorn School values of friendship and loyalty. We will ALL discuss this with Madame Shetland. Follow me."

Miss Hind stomped off, then turned back. "And bring that glorious disco ball with you."

The three friends exchanged glances. What was going to happen next . . . ?

They picked up the disco ball and raced through the corridors to stand outside the hall. Mira could see the room did look truly spectacular and was full of their friends and the other Unicorn School students having fun. Miss Hind was waiting at the door with Madame Shetland. They both looked very stern, despite their glittering, glamorous party

clothes. Miss Hind was still red in the face as she explained what a nice thing Mira and Raheem had done for their friend.

Madame Shetland nodded and crossed her arms. "Darcy, you deserved your detention. But taking responsibility so that all your classmates could go to the dance was the right thing to do. Have you learned your lesson?"

Darcy nodded.

"And Mira and Raheem," Madame Shetland continued. "You have taken a lot of risks these last few days, but it has been to help and support your friend."

Mira and Raheem nodded. Mira crossed her fingers behind her back.

Madame Shetland finally smiled. "Therefore, you have definitely adhered to Unicorn School Rule 64: Being a Loyal Friend Overrides Other Behavior on Certain Occasions. And, as such . . . You shall ALL go to the dance!"

"HOOORAAAAAY!" Mira and Darcy were yelling and high-fiving.

Miss Hind tapped Raheem on the shoulder. "Hurry up, Raheem! They need you in the lighting booth. And set up that disco ball right away."

Raheem grinned and trotted off with Brave.

When Mira and Darcy went into the hall, the whole of Class Red huddled around them, cheering loudly.

By the time Mira and Darcy had finished
hugging everyone, Raheem had set up the
disco ball. Then he switched on the lights.

The entire hall was lit with squillions of magical sparkles, as if the stars had come down from the sky and were shining just for the dance.

Just then, "Glitter Fever's Gonna Get You" came on the speakers, the crowd split, and Class Red ran onto the dance floor in two straight lines, children in front of unicorns.

"My routine!" Darcy squeaked.

Freya gave her a friendly punch on the shoulder and shouted over the music, "We've been practicing!" Then she ran to join Princess and her friends in the dance. As the lines parted, with each partner doing their very best jazz hands or hooves, Darcy launched herself right down the center, doing an endless spinning wheelie.

Mira laughed and felt a nudge. Dave was holding out a hoof. She giggled again and curtsied to him. "Why, yes, I will have this dance, thank you!" They had to dodge Rani and Angelica, who were doing the most incredible series of spinning lifts right across the hall. They looked so cool that people in their path stopped dancing to applaud them. Mira had never seen her sister look happier. She gave her a big thumbs-up.

Freya shimmied over to Mira and did a spin. She sniffed and made a funny face. Over the loud music, Freya

shouted into Mira's ear, "Does something smell weird?"

A small clump of hay coated in glittery unicorn poop fell off the disco ball onto Princess, and Mira quickly shouted back, "Let's go and get some punch!"

They danced over to the treats table and helped themselves to some rainbow cake and chocolate-dipped marshmallows. Flo asked Darcy if she liked the party.

"Well," Darcy said thoughtfully, "Jake didn't get the decorations exactly right, and the line dancing wasn't really—OW!"

Mira had poked Darcy in the ribs.

Darcy cleared her throat. "I mean," she said, "it's totally perfect. Come on, let's dance!"

They all pranced back onto the dance floor in their pairs. Dave slipped on a bit of disco-ball poop and managed to do the partner slide with jazz hooves that he'd found so hard in rehearsal!

Mira laughed and spun around her unicorn. It had been a very eventful few days at Unicorn School. But now she was disco dancing with Dave and all her best friends. It was . . .

AMAZING!

DAZZLING DANCE QUIZ

How much have YOU remembered about *Dave the Unicorn: Dance Party*?

1. What's the name of Mira and Rani's cat?
   a. Pom Pom
   b. Poppy
   c. Pickles

2. What's the first super-special treat Mira brings Dave in this book?
   a. Jelly doughnut
   b. Chocolate
   c. Strawberry licorice

3. What's the theme of the Unicorn School Dance?
   a. Glitz and Glamour
   b. Gardens
   c. Glitter Fever

4. Who is quest leader in this book?
   a. Flo
   b. Freya
   c. Jake

5. Raheem insists Brave wear this when they go into the Crystal Maze Mine . . .
   a. Protective face mask
   b. High-visibility jacket
   c. Safety helmet

6. What is School Rule 73?
   a. Always Be Kind to Your Unicorn
   b. Give Dave Plenty of Doughnuts
   c. Leave the Forest as You Find It

UNICORN JOKES

What did the mirror say to the unicorn?
I see u-nicorn.

Which unicorn always gets forgotten?
The who-nicorn.

Why didn't the skeleton go to the dance?
Because he had no body to go with!

What happened to the smallest unicorn?
He grew-nicorn.

What dance would a car do at the disco?
A brake dance.

Which unicorn is a ghost in disguise?
The boooooo-nicorn!

Dave and Mira's adventures are just beginning!
Escape Unicorn School with everyone's
favorite unicorn best friends in
Dave the Unicorn: Field Trip!

Turn the page for a sneak peek!

CHAPTER ONE
Tick Tock, Tick Tock

Tick tock, tick tock, BRRRRRRRRRRRRRR!

"Good morning, Rani!" said Mira, as her big sister opened her eyes.

"GGAAAARRRRRGH!" Rani screamed. "Why are you in my face?!"

Mira threw down the alarm clock and started jumping up and down on her sister's bed. "We've got to get to Unicorn School! It's MY FIELD TRIP TODAY!" Mira yelled. She was waving her signed permission slip in the air. "I'm almost ready! I just need to make my packed lunch."

"Get OFF!" Rani shoved Mira off the bed and stuck her head under the pillow.

Mira jumped onto the floor, hopping from foot to foot. "What do you think I should have in my sandwiches, tuna or cheese?"

"GO AWAY!" Rani flung a pillow at her little sister.

"Okay, bye! See you downstairs!" Mira dodged the pillow and scooped up their cat, Pickles, for a cuddle on the way.

Soon, she'd be cuddling Dave, her UBFF (Unicorn Best Friend Forever). He was the best unicorn in the world. Sure, he could be pretty grumpy. And he ALWAYS wanted to eat snacks or take a nap, and this often got them both

in trouble. And he certainly wasn't as glittery
as some of the other unicorns. (He was much
more farty.) BUT Dave was Mira's UBFF and
they always ended up having the most amazing
adventures and TONS of fun.

Unicorn School was Mira's favorite place in
the whole world. They went on quests around
the Fearsome Forest, hung out with Darcy and
Raheem and their unicorns, AND earned medals.
She couldn't wait to go back!

∪∪∪

After Mira had made her sandwiches (she'd
decided on cheese) and had some breakfast, it
was time to get dressed.

"I wish I could wear my kitticorn pajamas to

school, Pickles," Mira said, stroking the picture of

the adorable kitticorn on her PJs. A kitticorn was

a supercute baby cat that had a horn just like a

unicorn. She'd found a book about them in the

Unicorn School library and ever since then she'd

been OBSESSED—drawing tons of pictures of

them, keeping a list of her Top Ten Kitticorn Facts,

and making her very own kitticorn toy out of

cotton wool and a toilet paper

roll (even though Rani

said it looked

more like a

weird pig).

Mira was

longing to meet

a kitticorn in real life, but they were VERY rare. She was planning to ask the Unicorn School teachers if they'd ever seen one. But first she had to get to Unicorn School!

As soon as Mira and Rani were dressed, it was time to leave. Rani was still grumbling about having to get up so early, but Mira was so excited about her very first Unicorn School trip that she chatted nonstop in the car on the way to the Magic Portal, and all the way around the supermarket.

Most people brought their unicorns treats like hay or carrots. But Dave liked doughnuts best of all. Unfortunately the store didn't have any doughnuts, so Mira brought some vanilla cream cookies instead. She'd read that vanilla creams were a kitticorn's favorite food, and so she was sure Dave would like them, too! They were on sale, so she got five packages.

Mira checked and double-checked her bag for her packed lunch and permission slip. She didn't want anything to get in the way of her first field trip. She didn't even know where they were going yet! It was all so exciting.

When they arrived at the Magic Portal, it wasn't as busy as usual. It was only Mira's class, Class Red, who had a field trip and had to arrive super early. There was something extra special about being at the portal before most other people had gotten there, and before the sun was even fully up. It felt like going on vacation!

"Have a wonderful school trip, Mira!" said Mom, giving her a big hug, while Rani yawned loudly in her ear.

"Thanks, Mom. Oh look, there's Raheem!" Mira ran toward Raheem while waving back at her mom. "See you soooooooon!"

Raheem was one of Mira's best friends at Unicorn School. Along with Darcy, the three of them always had incredible adventures. Raheem was clutching his briefcase and looking a little bleary-eyed. Mira sprinted over and knocked him off-balance with a huge hug.

"Woohoo! Are you ready for this?!" she yelled in his ear.

"Um, yes, hello!" Raheem mumbled through a yawn.

"Then LET'S GO!" Mira dragged Raheem over to the portal, which was in some bushes behind the trash cans. On the way she listed her top five favorite kitticorn colors, to wake him up a little. When they reached the

bushes, Mira reached out for the sparkles
and—

ffffzzzzzz   **whumpfffff**

Twinkly lights exploded around them as they
zoomed upward, as if they were being sucked
up a spiral slide by a rainbow vacuum cleaner.
As quickly as they whooshed upward, they were
suddenly hurtling back down again. Soft pink
and gold rays of the rising sun shone in their eyes
as they tumbled onto the landing haystack and
rolled out into the Grand Paddock.

Mira took a deep breath and looked around.
Right away she spotted something new. Next to the
landing haystack was a big rainbow-colored BUS!

"Do you think that's for the field trip? I can't wait to find out where we're going!" Mira squealed, squeezing Raheem in excitement.

Just then, they heard a—

"TA-DAAA!" It was Darcy, spinning over to them with a wheelie. She gave Mira and Raheem high fives. "Hi, team. Missed you! Shall we find our—"

Before Darcy had a chance to finish, two unicorns came cantering over. Star and Brave were Darcy's and Raheem's unicorns, and today they were wearing the presents that Darcy and Raheem had made them on an earlier visit to Unicorn School. Brave was wearing Raheem's special homemade superhero cape,

while Star was in a wig that Darcy had made her
so they would have matching hair.

Star and Brave gave their humans a nuzzle. But
where was Dave?

Mira looked around for her Unicorn Best
Friend Forever. Down the hill, the school turrets
and clock tower gleamed in the rising sun.
Beyond the school, Mira could see the Fearsome
Forest, and beyond that the sparkly Crystal
Mountains. It was all so magical, but there was still
no sign of Dave.

Miss Glitterhorn, the Class Red teacher,
appeared by the side of the bus, yawning and
drinking from a very big mug of tea. She put the
tea down and clapped her hands.

"Good morning, Class Red!" she called.

"Gooooood mooooorrrning, Miss Glitterhorrrrn," called the children, sounding more tired than usual.

"Hi, Mom!" shouted Flo, who'd fallen asleep and woken up with a start.

"Please line up with your unicorns for the field trip," said Miss Glitterhorn. "We are leaving shortly. Have your permission slips ready!"

Mira quickly checked—yes, she still had her permission slip. But where was her unicorn? She didn't want him to miss the field trip!

"Dave? Da-ave!" Mira called quietly, ducking behind the bus to see if she could spot him.

Colin the Caretaker was filling up the bus with

rainbow-berry juice. The pump was attached
to a long line of tubes all coming from different
rainbow-berry trees at the edge of the forest.

Colin suddenly looked confused. He took
the pump out of the bus and shook it. It
looked like the juice had dried up.

There was a sudden *slurp* sound behind her. Mira looked around and saw a plump unicorn butt poking out of the rainbow-berry trees. *There* was her unicorn!

"Dave!" she whispered.

The little unicorn turned and gave her

a wave with his front hoof. He had one of the pipes in his mouth and was guzzling up the rainbow-berry juice!

"There you are!" Mira said with a giggle and ran over to give him a big hug.

By distracting Dave with a slightly sticky candy she found in her pocket, Mira managed to get the pipe off him and reconnect it to the pump. Colin started whistling happily as the juice began flowing into the bus again. Dave gave a series of cheerful burps.

"Dave, we have to line up with the others. We're going on a trip today!" Mira tried to wipe off the rainbow-berry stains from around Dave's mouth with the end of her sleeve, but she just ended up covered in the berry juice, too. "That's a bit better. Come on!"

Usually Mira had to drag Dave everywhere because he was either asleep or he would sit down and refuse to move. But right now Dave seemed very overexcited. Mira wondered if it was because of all the supersweet rainbow-berry juice and the toffee. Instead of just trotting back to the bus, Dave zoomed backward and forward across the grass, knocking into trees and still burping loudly. Then he started doing all his best prancing moves. Eventually Mira managed to push the little prancing unicorn around to the bus just as Miss Glitterhorn was crossing the last of her classmates off the register.

"And, good! That's everyone. Oh!" said Miss Glitterhorn. "Dave—you look . . . rather unusual this morning?"

Mira looked closely at her unicorn. His mane had turned rainbow-colored. It must have been the rainbow-berry juice!

"Um, Dave just wanted to . . . look nice for the field trip?" Mira said. She hoped her teacher wouldn't ask any more questions.

"How lovely," said Miss Glitterhorn vaguely.

Phew, thought Mira. Surely soon they would find out where they were going and then the field trip could begin!